ACPL ITEM
DISCARDED

J
COLLINGTON, PETER
THE COMING OF THE SURFMAN

W9-BVX-207

DO NOT REMOVE
CARDS FROM POCKET

MAR   1994

ALLEN COUNTY PUBLIC LIBRARY
FORT WAYNE, INDIANA 46802

You may return this book to any agency, branch,
or bookmobile of the Allen County Public Library.

DEMCO

THE COMING
OF THE SURFMAN

Peter Collington

Alfred A. Knopf
New York

There are two gangs in my neighborhood: the Hammers and the Nails. They are sworn enemies.

I was skateboarding home one day when the Hammer gang grabbed me. Their leader, Hammerhead, lifted me off the ground by my collar, pushed his face close to mine, and showed me his fist. "You're joining us," he said. It wasn't an invitation. It was a statement of fact. As I might want to smile again sometime–and it would be essential I had some teeth to do it with–I nodded.

"A wise decision," Hammerhead said, putting me down. "Now wear this." He handed me a red bandanna, the Hammers' color. As I walked away, struggling to put it around my head, I noticed the Nail gang up ahead. I quickly stuffed the bandanna into my pocket. Nailhead, the gang leader, looked me over. My foot tapped nervously on my skateboard. Nailhead's eyes lowered to my board.

"You wanna grow up. Skateboards are for kids." As I *was* a kid, it was quite logical that I should have a skateboard, but something made me keep quiet. It was my teeth again. Nailhead handed me a blue bandanna. "Wear this," he said. "You're one of us."

So I belong to two gangs, and if either of them finds out, I'm done for.

Allen County Public Library
900 Webster Street
PO Box 2270
Fort Wayne, IN 46801-2270

That night, I was lying awake thinking about my predicament when I heard a motor running. I looked out of my bedroom window and saw a van parked opposite, outside the boarded-up store. A man wearing beachwear stepped out. He looked around, the streetlight flashing on his sunglasses, and walked over to the store's front door. He jiggled with some keys and went in. He began unloading long cardboard cartons from his van.

After a while, I must have dropped off to sleep, but I was woken by the sound of an electric sander moaning and whining. The man had taken down the boards from the store window and was now working on the peeling paint.

The old store had closed down long ago because the owner was fed up with vandals breaking his windows and with neighborhood gangs harassing his customers. So a new store would be welcome.

The man had now opened some paint cans and was brightening up the woodwork. I couldn't wait until morning to find out what kind of a store it was going to be. A pizza place, a video rental shop— even a new food store would be fine. We wouldn't have to lug groceries from eight blocks away anymore.

Then my heart sank. I remembered the gangs and what they might do to me tomorrow.

When I got up and went outside, the two gangs were waiting for me. At least that's what I thought at first, but then I noticed they weren't looking at me but at the new store. The gangs stood well apart and were pointing to the window display. Both Hammerhead and Nailhead took turns laughing and their respective gangs imitated them. The name of the store, emblazoned in bright neon lights, was SURFING SUPPLIES. In the store window were surfboards and different types of surfing wear.

I began to laugh myself, partly out of relief that the gangs had forgotten about me and partly because I shared their amusement. It was quite simple. There was nowhere around here to surf. The beach was a two-day drive away.

Who would open a store selling surfing stuff in a run-down neighborhood like this? Only someone who was two bread rolls short of a picnic. Someone who was seriously weird. The gangs laughed, and I laughed with them.

The SURFING SUPPLIES store opened regularly at nine o'clock every morning and closed at five-thirty on the dot. No one went into the store to buy anything, and no one came out.

The store owner became known as the Surfman, and people hooted and laughed whenever his name was mentioned. I didn't know what to think, but I was glad about one thing. Since he had come, the Hammers and Nails had forgotten entirely about me and hardly fought each other anymore. The blank, angry stares were gone; expression was leaking into their faces. I had seen that look before—especially in cats. It was a look of obsessive curiosity. Their brains were straining to figure out why the Surfman was here. Anyone weird could also be dangerous. So both gangs set up around-the-clock surveillance.

A pattern of behavior was emerging. Every Monday morning the Surfman cleaned his windows and swept the sidewalk. Once a month he took stock, even though he had sold nothing. High-intensity binoculars revealed that he ate a mixed salad and yogurt for lunch and ran 200 miles a week on his exercise machine. He *had* to be training for something—but what?

Then one night I spotted him. He came out of his store about eleven o'clock and walked over to the abandoned factory across the way. He took out a large piece of paper and studied it by flashlight. He looked up at the factory and then down at the sheet of paper. He walked around the factory for a while and then went back to the store.

After this, the Surfman started appearing regularly at night, carrying a tool kit. He had more in common with the gangs than I had at first thought: he was very good at wrecking things. He was systematically demolishing the factory. It was crazy. Each night there was hammering and banging for hours on end. But as the weeks went by, there seemed to be some method in his madness.

With the help of the old factory crane, the Surfman ripped off the factory roof and sent the metal sheets crashing down onto the floor below. Then he began bolting the sheets onto the inner walls and floor. His long shadow spilled out over the ground as the light from his welding equipment flickered and darted. The Surfman rolled large pipes from the back of the factory and collected them together by the pump. Then he started bolting them together.

At the end of his night shift, he would stagger home, tired and drained, but he always opened the store, regular as clockwork, at nine o'clock, even though no one had ever seen a customer go in.

I began to really feel for him. He reminded me of my late dad, always working hard and no one giving him any thanks.

3 1833 02402 6434

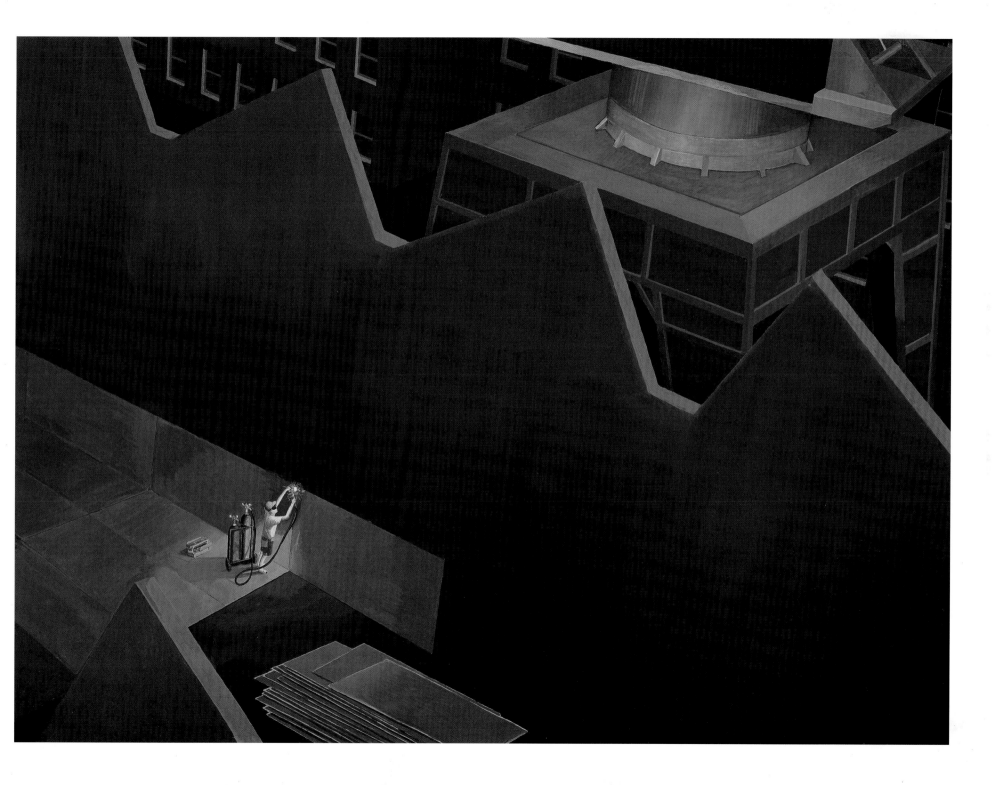

One evening, the Surfman erected scaffolding in front of the two giant storage tanks and, with cutting equipment, began burning into the metal. Every night something new was added or changed, and in the light of day the two gangs would check out the Surfman's progress. Occasionally, the gangs would take turns flexing their muscles and knocking something down. But their hearts weren't really in it, and when the Surfman repaired the damage, they just shrugged and let things stand.

They, like me, wanted to see the Surfman complete his work. We were all enthralled. We were trembling with anticipation. We all knew what the Surfman was building, but nobody put it into words. The Surfman jokes had died away, and a certain grudging respect was apparent. He might be a weird guy, but he was a weird guy who was making something for us. Something we had wanted all our lives.

One night, I was woken by the sound of running water. The Surfman was standing by the metal pipes turning a large wheel tap. He was wearing swimwear. As he pressed a switch, the pump started throbbing and vibrating. The Surfman picked up his surfboard and climbed high up the metal ladder to a position overlooking the empty factory below. He leaned forward and pulled a lever. The doors of the two storage tanks sprang open, and WATER gushed out with all the ferocity of a giant surfing wave! The Surfman was swept from his perch, only to reappear with his surfboard under his feet and his arms stretched out on either side. *The Surfman was surfing!* He rode the wave all the way to the end of the factory, was carried up the metal slope, and then plummeted ski-slope-style onto the piled-up car tires below.

   The Surfman retrieved his surfboard and clambered down the tires. With his surfboard under his arm, he walked over to his store and went in. The wave machine wheezed and coughed, then spluttered to a halt. I always knew what it was going to be, but now I screamed the words out loud: "It's a WAVE MACHINE!" My voice echoed out of the window and ricocheted around the neighborhood. I heard whoops and cries of joy from Hammerhead and Nailhead, who had witnessed it too.

   Tomorrow was going to be a great day.

In the morning, the two gangs were there early, clutching bits of wood and anything else they thought might do for a surfboard. When the wave machine started up, the gangs clambered up the ladder and, mixing together like one happy family, launched themselves and their bits of wood onto the wave. I just stood and watched. This was going to be fun. None of them had the slightest idea of how to surf, so they sank with their bits of wood and came up with furious faces, spurting water.

I had been saving up money for some time, not quite sure what to do with it. Now, I *knew!* As my dad used to say, "To do the job right, you need the right tool."

I walked over to the SURFING SUPPLIES store and put down my money. The Surfman handed me a real beauty of a board. He wasn't a talkative sort of guy. But as I left, he turned and said, "Have a good day."

I walked over to the wave machine and climbed up the stairs. The gangs stood back to watch. I waited until I heard the crash of water, and as the wave came, I stepped off. All that skateboarding had been good training. I held my balance and rode the crest of the wave for all it was worth. It was the best day of my life. The gangs tried to follow my example, but they had no balance, and their boards were rubbish. They knew what they had to do.

Nailhead led his gang in first. They all bought surfboards and walked proudly out of the Surfman's store. Next, Hammerhead led his gang into the store. When the Hammers came out, Nailhead was there to confront them. He swallowed hard. The words did not come easy to him.

"You wanna have a truce?" he asked.

Hammerhead looked back at his gang. They all nodded their heads. "Okay," said Hammerhead. "We surf alternate days." He held out his hand to shake.

"Done," said Nailhead.

The two gangs beamed at each other.

Nailhead took out a coin. "Heads or tails?"

Nailhead and his gang won the toss, and cheering, they ran over to the wave machine to try out their boards.

I put on my blue bandanna and joined them. The next day, I put on my red bandanna and joined the Hammers.

After a week, they found me out. I was thrown out of both gangs, and my surfing days were over. All I could do now was watch. I felt bored and depressed. Without surfing, life felt almost not worth living.

One day, I was enviously watching one of the gangs surfing when the pump suddenly ground to a halt. A cry of pain went up from every gang member's throat. The wave machine had broken down.

That evening, the Surfman came out of his shop and called me over. He handed me his tool kit, and I walked behind him over to the wave machine. I handed him each tool as he requested it, and when the job was finished, he turned to me and said, "Okay, try it out." I ran home and got my surfboard. I couldn't believe my luck. I tried one wave, curling down its crest and zigzagging in front of it.

"How is it?" called the Surfman.

"Almost right," I answered. "I'll just check it out again." And this way I got to surf a second time—a long time—until I felt I was stretching the Surfman's patience and finally called out, "Yeah, it's fine now!" And the Surfman closed it down until the next day.

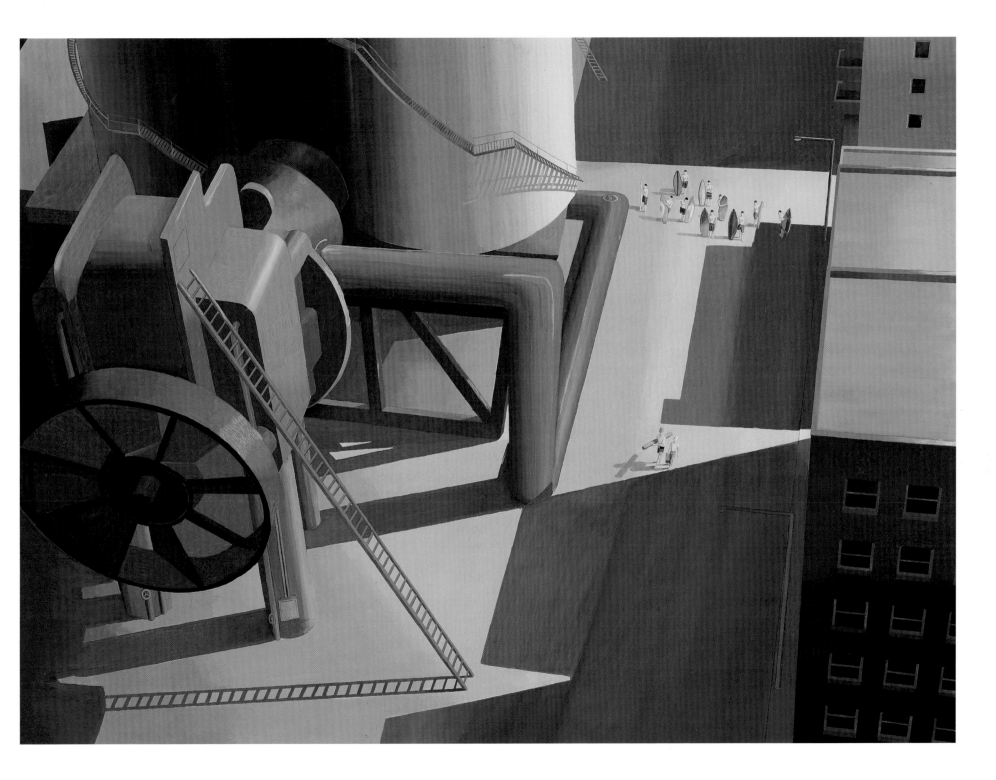

Fortunately, the wave machine broke down quite regularly, and I was always on hand to carry the Surfman's tool kit. As he worked, he talked to me, explaining what he was doing and why. He named each tool I handed to him as if he wanted me to remember what it was for the next time. The Surfman really did remind me of my late dad: *he* always liked to have me stand by him when he was fixing things. But I did the same thing now that I used to do with my dad. I humored him. I nodded and said "Yeah" a few times as if I were paying attention. But my mind wasn't there. It was focused on surfing and silently crying out for that moment when the Surfman would turn to me and say, "Okay, it's fixed. Go try it out." Then life for me would begin. Floating on those short-lived waves was everything to me.

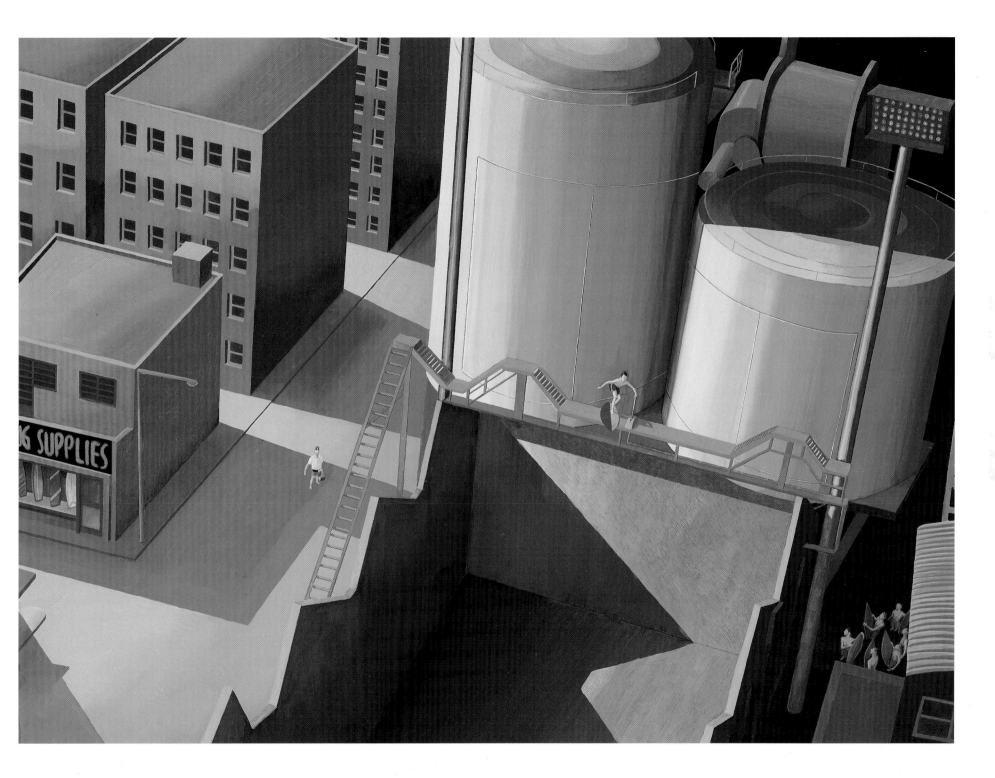

On their enforced day of rest, while one gang surfed, the other spent its time jogging to the health food store in the next neighborhood for more supplies or sitting around watching surfing movies they had rented from the Surfman's store, analyzing and discussing good moves.

Then the truce broke down. The wave machine had been out of action for a whole day, so the Hammers felt they should surf the next day. The Nails insisted it was their turn, and fighting broke out. The Hammers, anticipating trouble, had come prepared. They had hidden their own surfboards, and producing axes and sledge-hammers, they rushed over to the Nails' surfboards and began smashing them.

The result was catastrophic. The Nails let out agonizing screams of pain and doubled over on the ground, hugging the remains of their surfboards. They clutched them like babies and went home brokenhearted to try and fix them. The Hammers felt powerful—they had never been happier. They surfed all that day, confident that they would be surfing every day from now on.

But somehow I knew that would not be the end of it.

That night, I was woken by the sound of banging and crashing. Looking out of my bedroom window, I saw the Nail gang wielding axes and sledgehammers. They were smashing the wave machine. I quickly dressed and ran out to try and stop them. But it was too late. The Hammer gang was there too, and a big battle was taking place. I shouted and tried to reason with them, but no one took any notice of me. Water was spurting out of the pipes, and sparks were flying everywhere.

The following day, the two battle-weary and dejected gangs stood in front of the wave machine and looked at the damage they had caused. Their eyes looked over toward the Surfman's store. He had fixed things before. Surely he would fix things again.

Later that evening, I watched the Surfman walk out of his store and across to the battered wave machine. He stood for some time, just shaking his head. Then he walked home and into his store.

The next morning the Surfman had gone. His store was empty and the wave machine unrepaired. The two gangs stood in silence. Big tears rolled down their faces.

I ran back home to get my late dad's tool kit. The two gangs stepped aside to let me work. I tried various tools, pulling this way and that. But I knew in my heart it was hopeless. I couldn't remember what the Surfman had told me. I hadn't been listening. The gangs' hopeful eyes narrowed.

"Stupid kid," they said, and walked away.

Things have gone pretty much back to normal here, the gangs once again fighting each other. Neither of them is interested in my joining them now, which is fine with me.

On bad days, I think about my father a lot and all the things I could have done with him if he were still alive. On good days, I feel sure that the Surfman will return, and this time I know I'll be ready and really listen to what he says and really watch his big hands as he works away at the rusting hulk of the wave machine, restoring it to good working order.

THIS IS A BORZOI BOOK PUBLISHED BY ALFRED A. KNOPF, INC.

Copyright © 1993 by Peter Collington

All rights reserved under International and Pan-American Copyright Conventions. Published in
the United States of America by Alfred A. Knopf, Inc., New York, and simultaneously in Canada
by Random House of Canada Limited, Toronto. Distributed by Random House, Inc., New York.
Originally published in Great Britain in 1993 by Jonathan Cape Ltd., an imprint of Random House
UK Ltd. First American edition 1994.

Library of Congress Cataloging-in-Publication Data

The coming of the surfman / by Peter Collington.
p. cm.
Summary: When the Surfman comes to a rundown neighborhood torn by gang warfare
to open an unusual business, he brings peace for a while—but only a while.
ISBN 0-679-84721-9 [1. Gangs—Fiction. 2. Surfing—Fiction] I. Title.
PZ7.C686Co 1993 92-41844 [Fic]—dc20

Manufactured in Hong Kong
2 4 6 8 0 9 7 5 3 1